The
Poison

Nikki's

Sisters of vengeance

Introduction

"Blood is thicker
than water until
they mix, that's

why betrayal is like a river of blood in the rain being washed away in the dead of night, it's funny, dying in the rain tonight when I was born in the rain not that many nights ago". My name is Nicolette Poinsettia, legend has it my family name comes from my great great grandmother who used the Poinsettia plant to make poison she then used to kill a group of men that killed her husband. As the story goes, during that time

period there was so
much racial tension
and since my great
great grandmother
was a Belosian
woman and her
husband a
Negarza, their
union was not only
seen as illegal at the
time but immoral
and evil to mix

races, the punishment for such and unholy union was death. One night when my great great grand parents were out for a stroll they were attacked by a group of Belosian men, they were both beaten half to death and my great great grandfather was held down and forced to watch as they raped his wife, when their appetite for vile cruelty was satiated they killed him and left my great great grandmother for dead, but she didn't die, and it wouldn't be long before she had her revenge. Using her knowledge of plants and herbs as well as what her husband taught her of Nivenou, a spiritual practice all Papalitos and Mayalitas must learn in order to control Niven and harness Nivenity, she formulated a poison that would not only kill her targets but curse their bloodlines, at the center of this cursed formula was the bright red Poinsettia, no one

knows for sure why
she chose a plant
that on its own isn't
very harmful,
maybe for its color
or even perhaps its
chemical makeup
was necessary for
the mixture, what
we do know is the
poison worked.
One by one she

tracked the men down, poison ground to a fine powder in her hand and all it took was a breath, once she blew the red dust their way they were sentenced to death, all it needed to do was touch them, simply making

contact with their
skin spelled the
end, but going
home, well thats
what cursed them,
you see this poison
acted more like a
virus infecting its
host and killing
them slowly as well
as infecting those
they come in

contact with, within
a few short weeks
half the town was
either sick or dying,
their symptoms
were all the same, a
burning sensation
as if there whole
body was on fire,
abscesses and open
wounds forming on
their skin and

bleeding from every orifice on their body. One of her attackers realizing he was cursed decided to confess his vens to a priest, yet instead of being condemned for his crimes, my great great grand mother was called a

"Vermaya" or Witch in todays misunderstanding of mythology, you see back before there was any fiction novels or pop culture, people had deeper connections to the supernatural realms and occult Nyince,

what we call
witches today, have
been, still are, and
will always be
Vermaya, who are
Mayalitas who
have chosen to
walk the path of
evil, Vermpatrio
are Papalitos who
have chosen that
same path,

translated these titles are mother or father of vermin, the Vermaya were said to be given power over these creatures as well as the power to corrupt the Nivenity and flesh of mankind by exploiting the vens within peoples hearts and minds for their master Sedeneve. Perhaps the most infamous Vermaya was Mercillisa Witch who lived during the 15th century, her power wasn't the greatest by old standards or new,

however the public
nature of her death
would be the
catalyst for the
birth of generations
of Vermaya both
real and fake alike,
and these new
Vermaya would be
named after her
and called witches.
Before Mercillisa,

hunters trained in
the occult would
track down and kill
Vermaya in secret
and for centuries
no one knew these
creatures existed,
until one day in
order to escape a
hunters grasp
Mercillisa turned to
the people of her

town, playing the victim and convincing everyone the hunter was a mad man who tried to rape and kill her, at first it worked like a charm, the hunter was imprisoned and scheduled for execution, however after pleading his case and reminding the towns folk of all the strange occurrences that have been plaguing them, attention turned towards Mercillisa, and the very first unsanctioned witch trial was held, and

with all his
knowledge of
Vermaya it was
easy to convince
the towns folk of
the truth, and
Mercillisa Witch
was burned at the
stake, whispers
spread, and rumors
became legend,
and before long the

witch was
everyones worst
nightmare, so when
people started to
question if their
were more like her,
it was only natural
they would call
these creatures by
her name, thus the
witch became a
household name.

So like so many others that came before her my great great grand mother was burned at the stake like a witch, but she was no witch, nor Vermaya, she was a Mayalita till the very end, her Nivenity was pure, and her motives were just, luckily for my great grandmother and her siblings, they were able to flee with their aunt, however to avoid being hunted and killed for being descendants of a witch, they had to

change their
surname in order to
go into hiding, my
great grandmother
chose the name of
the bright red plant
she watched her
mother use to
create her cursed
poison, and ever
since my family
name has been

Poinsettia. This is my story, how a girl with poison in her veins and a cursed past became a dark hero in a city on the verge of damnation, oh yeah, I also become a total rockstar.

Episode 1
Broken Mirror

Thinking back now about how my journey began, I was so naive, 18 years old, fresh out of high school all I could think about is following my dream, boy was I fearless. I grew up in a small town called Willow Haven just outside of SkyGuard City, as a kid I always dreamed of moving to the City and becoming a rockstar, so as soon as I graduated from high school it was time to put small town life behind me. I didn't think twice hopping on the first train to SkyGuard, my parents weren't to thrilled at the idea but after 18 years of them raising me they knew exactly how strong willed I am, they also knew I would be staying with and old friend I knew since kindergarten, Victoria Kellar and her parents, who were our next door neighbors back when they lived in Willow Haven. Even though it had been 3 years since I saw Vicky she was like a sister to me, we shared the same dream of starting a band and becoming famous rockstars, so when she had to move away to SkyGuard City for her fathers job, I wasn't sad, I just knew it was fate and that one day when I was old enough to leave home I would come to the City, find her, and we would take over the world. When I made it to the City I was in awe just at the train station, everything was so congested there were people everywhere you turned, I admit I began to feel a little bit like a fish out of water, and that's when I heard her voice, my best friend whom I only been able to keep in touch with by phone for the past 3 years was right behind me, calling my name as if we had never been apart, for a second I wondered how does she even recognize me? When I turned around though, the mystery was solved, as soon as I saw her I realized how much we stood out, everyone around us was dressed so casual yet the two of us looked like we were fresh out of a punk rock music video, I couldn't help it, heck we both couldn't, we ran into each others arms as if we were trying to tackle each other.

Nikki P. "Oh my Nag, I can't believe its you its been forever"

Vicky. "Tell me about it, its been 3 years since we made a pact that when we finished high school we would start our music journey together"

Nikki P. "Look at us now, so far from those little girls with their heads in the clouds, we're grown women with the world at our feet"

Vicky. "Grown women? You still look like the same little girl who didn't make the cheerleading team because you didn't have enough curves, guess you never filled out"

Nikki P. "Look who's talking, I should call Ripley's believe it or not, because I clearly found the worlds tallest 10 year old"

Vicky. "Say what you like, but this is the body of a seductress"

We couldn't stop laughing, after 3 years we really didn't change much, one major change though, was we weren't kids anymore, it was time to stop dreaming and start living.

Nikki P. "Gosh, I can't wait to see this City, you have to take me everywhere, I wanna see it all"

Vicky. "Trust me your gonna get to see the City, but first lets get you home so you can unpack"

Nikki P. "Home? Vicky do you know what that means?"

Vicky. "Heck yeah"

Nikki P. "I totally live in SkyGuard City, and we're totally freaking roommates"

It was happening, the dream was coming true, the whole drive back to Vickys house I fought back tears of joy staring out the window at this huge amazing City that I could now call my home. When we arrived at the house it was like a tornado had touched down, we blew through the house like excited school girls, I barely got to say hello to Vickys parents, and before I could even settle in we dropped my luggage in Vickys room and headed back out to drive around the city.

Nikki P. "So where are we heading first? A club? A bar? How about the mall? There are so many places to choose"

Vicky. "Easy tiger, we have plenty of time for you to explore the city, we

have business to take
care of"

Nikki P. "Business?"

Vicky. "Yeah, you
wanna be a rockstar
right? I mean, I'm a
great drummer and
your and ok singer
but thats hardly a
band"

Nikki P. "True, what we need is more band members"

Vicky. "Bingo, what did you think I was doing for 3 years just waiting around for you to think of and answer to that question? You already know that I have been going to a preforming arts high school here in SkyGuard, what I never told you is I found 3 totally awesome chicks for the band"

Nikki P. "I'm crushed, you've been keeping secrets from me?"

Vicky. "Very funny, the only reason I

never filled you in is because I figured you would want to meet them and judge them for yourself"

Nikki P. "I can't wait to meet them, they better be epic"

It wasn't long until we pulled into the Pink Cherry Diner, this place was iconic, a complete staple of SkyGuard City, some of the biggest names in acting, music, modeling, everyone who's anyone has come here when visiting the city, this was definitely the best place to meet these mystery girls, besides, you can tell a lot about people by what they eat. Sitting down with these girls started off pretty awkward, I mean we're girls, we needed a moment to size each other up, it didn't help that Vicky just sat there and didn't even think to introduce us as if we all already knew each other, then there was the waitress Cathy, who was clearly new to her job and made things even more awkward, but she did break the ice.

Cathy. "Hi, I'm Cathy and I'll be your waitress today, you girls look like you must be Rock fans"

Tiffany Cook.

"Actually Cathy, we're rockstars, the names Tiffany Cook, this is Lisa Santana, Yuki Masumoto, Victoria Kellar, and our newest addition, I believe Vicky said her name was Nikki?"

Cathy. "I apologize, I grew up in a small town and just recently moved here, and honestly to tell you the truth I don't know much about rock'n'roll"

Tiffany Cook.
"Don't worry about it, you see we aren't famous yet, but if our new singer can sing as good as we jam, we're golden"

Tiffany Cook, cocky, conceited, arrogant, translation, I liked her from the gate.

Cathy. "I'll be sure to keep and eye out for you girls, so what will you all be having?"

Lisa Santana. "Coffee, Black"

Cathy. "Any sugar?"

Lisa Santana. "Salt"

Cathy. "Salt?"
Lisa Santana. "Salt"

Cathy. "Um, ok and for the rest of you?"

Yuki Masumoto. "I'll have the Grave

Digger deluxe burger, chunky cheese fries and a Pink Cherry milkshake"

Lisa Santana, dark mysterious, aloof, then there was Yuki Masumoto, a total foodie like me, yeah, I liked them too.

Cathy. "Anything else?""

Nikki P. "I'll have what she's having"

Cathy. "So two Grave Digger Deluxe Burgers"

Vicky. "I'll have a banana milkshake"

Tiffany Cook. "I'll have a salad"

Cathy. "What kind of salad?"

Tiffany Cook. "Surprise me"

It wasn't long before we were all swapping stories about how we became interested in music and how much being a rockstar meant to us. Tiffany Cooks mother was a classical pianist and like most parents she decided before Tiffany was born that she would follow in her footsteps, the good news was Tiffany grew to love playing music, the bad news is she loved playing it on a keyboard. Lisa Santana and Yuki Masumoto grew up together and went to the same middle & High school, however the first time they met was when Lisa's dad brought her into Yuki's fathers pawn shop to buy a guitar for her brother, she had been crying

because when she
asked her father to get
her a guitar too, he
told her, girls don't
play guitar because its
not lady like, Yuki's
story was similar, her
dad didn't want
anything getting in
the way of her studies
and forbid her to even
practice music, luckily
they never allowed
their dreams to be

crushed and continued to both practice in secret. Thinking back, me and Vickys Stories weren't that complicated, I grew up singing in the church and when I told my parents about my dream they pretty much supported me, and Vickys dad used to be in a small time rock band so he was thrilled when his daughter asked him to teach her to play the drums, it was shocking meeting girls that had to fight to be who they were, when me and Vicky could always be ourselves. It had only been a few hours talking and eating with these girls yet I knew they were the ones, I had never even thought of having an all girl band before, heck, way back when all I thought I needed was me and Vicky, but this felt right, I couldn't explain it, but I'm sure we all felt it.

Tiffany Cook. "So are you coming to the

battle of the bands tonight?"

Nikki P. "Definitely, it sounds like fun"

Lisa Santana. "It's not, it's homework, you need to see our competition first hand"

Vicky. "Once a month the Arrow Head club does a battle of the bands featuring the top bands in the city"

Nikki P. "How do you qualify?"

Yuki Masumoto. "In order to make it

into the battle of the bands, you gotta build your bands rep by playing small gigs at local clubs leading up to battle of the bands, if your picked you'd know by seeing your band name Xkripted on the S train"

Nikki P.
"Xkripted?"

Yuki Masumoto. "Xkripture is an ancient form of communicating through writings, drawings, sounds and songs etc all coded to hide information"

Nikki P. "Ok, I think I get it now, but why the S train specifically?"

Vicky. "Xkripture can be found all over, but Xkriptors have their favorite spots when posting bulletins, locals have dubbed the S train the train to success because the info posted on it mainly pertains to entertainment"

A feeling of excitement began to fill up inside of me like a fire, I felt I could explode, this city was so amazing and my dream was so close. With only a few hours till battle of the bands we decided to drive around the city so I could see how Xkripting works first hand. It wasn't long

before I could see just
how complex the city
was, it was as if there
were two cities
existing on top of
each other, driving
through different
neighborhoods, one
minute you were in a
lush metropolis and
the next you were in
the slums, Xkripture
connected the two
worlds together, by

translating these complex Xkriptures, you could find out anything, from what gangs were at war, to local jobs that were hiring, even deeper information was concealed within the hidden messages if you knew where to look, but some info could only be accessed with specific

Xkript keys that changed frequently and were only known by those who needed to know. My mind was racing, there was so much information to take in, and before we knew it, it was time to head to the battle of the bands. As the sun began to set the outer shell of the city gave way to its inner truth, a cold chill swept through the air, and the city that hours earlier felt safe and peaceful, now felt dangerous and frightening. When we reached the club it had began to rain, and even though it was pouring down, the line to get in was down the block, and parking was nowhere to be found so we had to drive eleven blocks away just to park. As we walked in the rain towards the club I couldn't shake this feeling that something big was going to happen, and our lives would be changed forever, and then, there was a scream, we all stopped in our tracks, frozen as if

time had stopped.
The scream could
only be described as
primal, like and
animal who knew it
was about to be
devoured was
screaming out in and
attempt to scare off its
attackers.

Vicky. "What the
hell was that?"

Yuki Masumoto. "Sounded like a girl"

Tiffany Cook. "It sounded like it came from up ahead"

Lisa Santana. "We should check it out, someone could need our help"

Tiffany Cook. "Check it out and end up in the same

position whoever screamed is in?"

Yuki Masumoto. "Wouldn't you want someone to check it out if it were you?"

Everyone was nervous, hell I was scared out of my

mind, but something in me took over, I had to answer this girls cry for help. My body began to move on its own, before I even realized it I had ran over towards where the screams were coming from. Standing there in the rain, knee deep in whatever trouble I had just gotten myself

into, I saw her, down
a dark alley. Beaten,
bleeding, with her
clothes torn, half
naked in the rain,
crying as her attackers
turned to look at me,
it was so dark, but as
lighting flashed over
head their images
were burned into my
memory, their eyes
glared at me, my
heart was pounding

but my fear was outweighed by the fact I needed to help, so I screamed at them to leave her alone, I wasn't thinking, there wasn't any time to think, I was only reacting in the moment. The men turned their attention to me walking toward me while fixing their pants, I was frozen, I don't know what would have happened if Vicky and the girls didn't rush over to me. Once the guys saw how many of us there were they decided to turn around and run away. As the guys ran the other way down the alley, me and the girls were able to run over to their victim, I could

only stand over her as
Vicky got down on
the ground to hold
her, Lisa stood watch
looking in the
direction the guys ran,
Yuki and Tiffany tried
helping to fix her
clothes, and yet I
couldn't do anything,
I could only watch
thinking to myself
why no one was
mentioning that the

girl in front of us, was Cathy, our waitress. Hours, just hours ago she was at work, she was happy and bubbly, now she was laying on the ground face beaten and bruised, bleeding and crying, I wondered if I was the only one who remembered her, I wondered if she remembered us, this girl, who was from a small town just like me, who just moved to this city just like me, this girl was like a mirror, a broken mirror reflecting my worst fear, my fear that no matter how strong and fearless I am, I'm still just a girl, and at any moment a guy bigger and stronger than me could reduced me to this, this broken victim.

Vicky. "Nikki, snap out of it, we have to get Cathy to a hospital"

And like that, I realized, they remembered, we all

did, they weren't ignoring the fact we met her hours earlier, they were working so hard to help because of that fact, because deep down we all felt the same thing when we looked at her, it could have been any of us.

To be continued…